AF066759

COLOUR BLINDNESS

BY ROBIN TWIDDY

A DIFFERENT WORLD

BookLife PUBLISHING

©2020
BookLife Publishing Ltd.
King's Lynn
Norfolk PE30 4LS
All rights reserved.
Printed in Malaysia.

A catalogue record for this book is available from the British Library.

ISBN: 978-1-83927-043-7

Written by:
Robin Twiddy

Edited by:
John Wood

Designed by:
Gareth Liddington

This book was written and designed with accessibility for people with colour vision deficiency and dyslexia in mind.

Look out for these banners throughout the book to see how different people see the world.

KEY:

Red-green colour blindness

Full-colour vision

Photo credits:

Cover & Throughout – CkyBe, Serhii Bobyk, Evgenii Emelianov, LauraKick, avian, Aleksandrs Bondars, 4&5 – ESB Professional, goir, 6&7 – galichstudio, FamVeld, 8&9 – Rio AbajoRio, paulaphoto, 10&11 – dezignor, d13, 12&13 – Victoria Shapiro, 14&15 – Farosofa, Phakamat BL, 16&17 – Kzenon, Germanova Antonina, Neveshkin Nikolay, VitaminCo, 18&19 – matimix, 20&21 – Dan Kosmayer, Sergey Novikov, 22&23 – Parilov, wavebreakmedia. Images are courtesy of Shutterstock.com. With thanks to Getty Images, Thinkstock Photo and iStockphoto.

All facts, statistics, web addresses and URLs in this book were verified as valid and accurate at time of writing. No responsibility for any changes to external websites or references can be accepted by either the author or publisher.

CONTENTS

Page 4	A Different World?
Page 6	What Is Colour Blindness?
Page 8	Red-Green Colour Blindness
Page 10	Are We Watching the Same Film?
Page 12	Inside the Eye
Page 14	Telling the Difference at the Market
Page 16	Made with Colour Blindness in Mind
Page 18	Which Team?
Page 20	Other Types of Colour Blindness
Page 22	Support
Page 24	Glossary and Index

Words that look like this can be found in the glossary on page 24.

A Different World?

We all live in the same world, don't we? Well, for some people who have a condition known as colour blindness, the world can look very different.

In this book you will have the chance to see what the world looks like for someone with colour blindness. It is important to understand how others see the world and the challenges they face.

What is Colour Blindness?

A better term is colour vision <u>deficient</u>, which just means a person sees fewer colours rather than not seeing any colours at all.

People with colour blindness have eyes that work a little differently to other people's eyes. People with colour blindness have trouble seeing some colours and mix others up.

Most people who have colour blindness have the red-green type of colour blindness and most of them are male. Very few people have total colour blindness. There are three types of colour blindness:

Red-green colour blindness

Blue-yellow colour blindness

Total colour blindness

Around 1 in 12 men have some amount of colour blindness.

Red-Green Colour Blindness

> Any colour can be made by mixing the three primary colours: yellow, red and blue.

Full colour wheel

Red-green colour blind colour wheel

Even though it is known as red-green colour blindness, many other colours are affected by it. Any colour that is made by mixing red or green with another colour will look different to someone with red-green colour blindness.

If you have red-green colour blindness, your eyes might have trouble seeing the colour red or the colour green. You might have trouble seeing both of those colours.

Are we watching the same film?

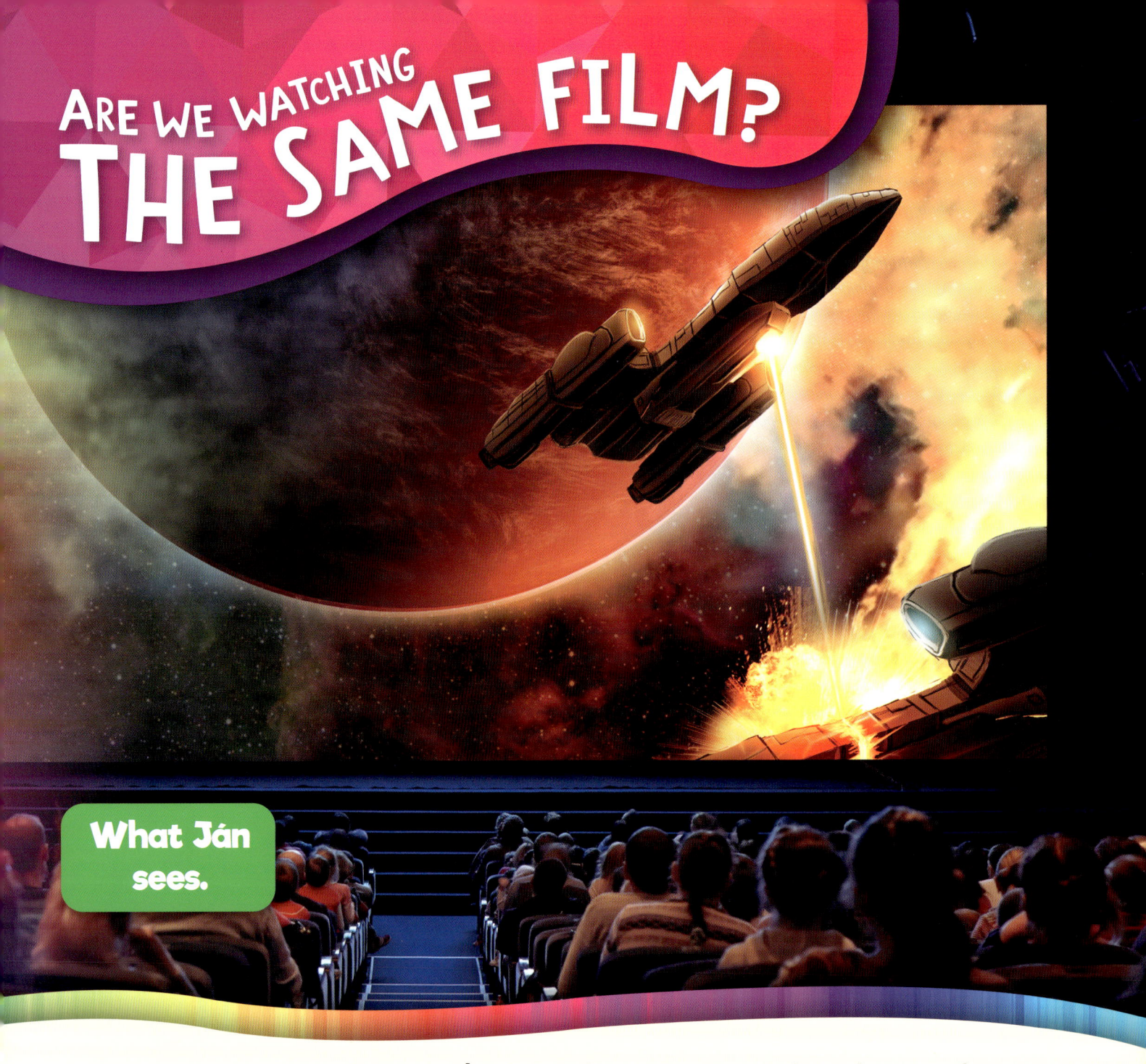

What Ján sees.

Adam and his best friend Ján love the cinema. Adam has red-green colour blindness and Ján does not. Are they watching the same film?

Adam has always had red-green colour blindness, and the way he sees the world is normal to him. However, sometimes when he is watching a film, his colour blindness can make it difficult to tell what is happening.

What Adam sees.

Inside the Eye

The cone cells are switched on by different colours.

Inside our eyes are special things called cone cells. There are three types of cone cell and each one helps us to see a different colour. One sees red, one sees green and one sees blue.

The brain knows which colour it is seeing by which cone cells are switched on. If the green cone cell isn't working, then the brain isn't told that it is seeing green.

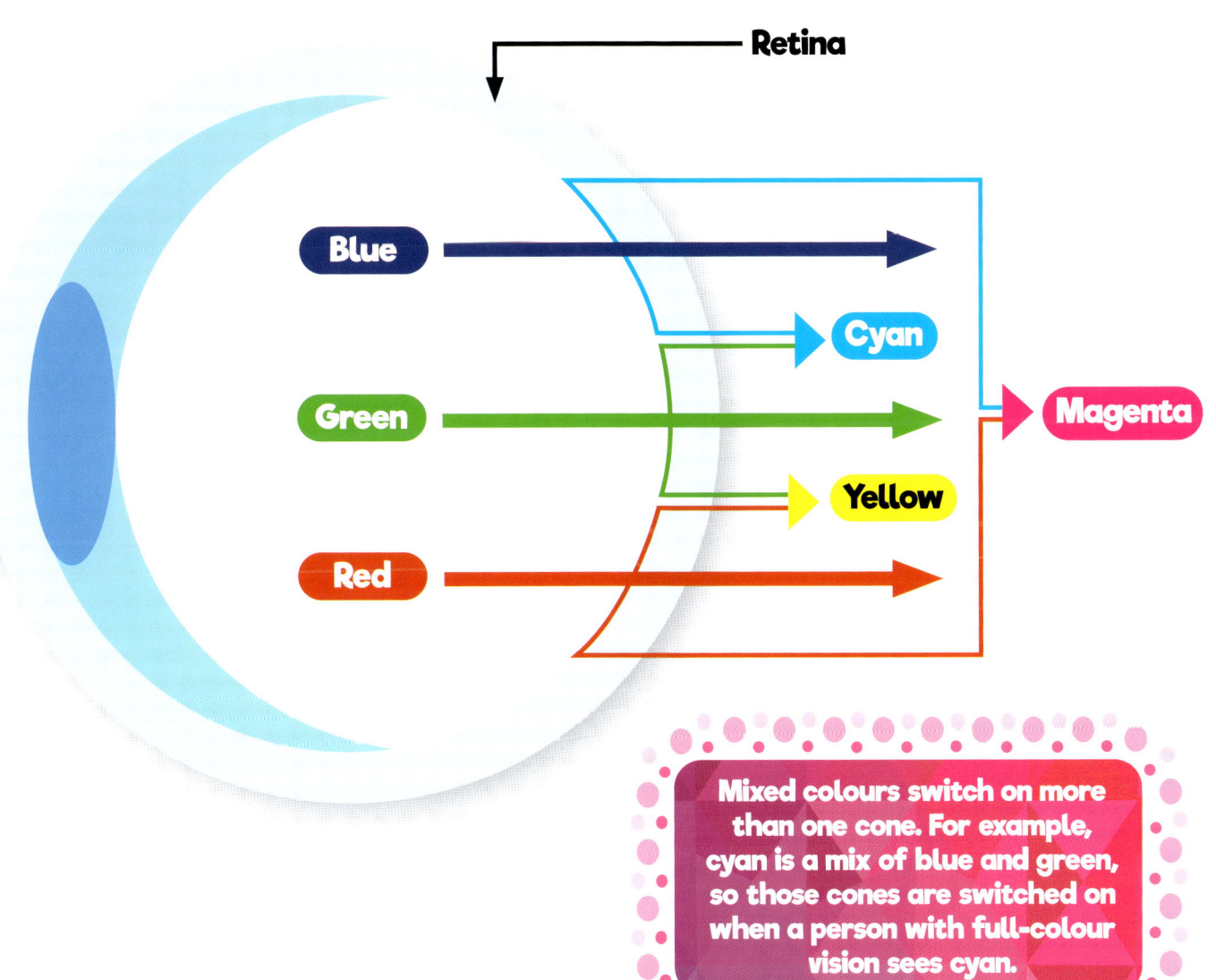

Mixed colours switch on more than one cone. For example, cyan is a mix of blue and green, so those cones are switched on when a person with full-colour vision sees cyan.

Telling the Difference at the Market

For some people with red-green colour blindness, it is hard to tell the difference between chocolate sauce and tomato sauce!

What Adam's dad sees.

Not being able to tell certain colours apart can sometimes make life tricky. When Adam goes to the market with his dad, Adam's colour blindness makes it hard to tell which fruit is ripe.

Many fruits change colour when they are ready to eat. Adam's dad doesn't have colour blindness, so he knows that the yellow bananas are ripe and the green bananas aren't. Adam cannot tell which are green and which are yellow.

What Adam sees.

For Adam, all the bananas are yellow. Can you tell which bananas are ready to eat?

MADE WITH COLOUR BLINDNESS IN MIND

Designers can use different **textures**, patterns, letters, numbers and symbols to make coloured items clearly different for the colour blind.

A lot of things in our world use colour to tell them apart, such as the pieces in a boardgame, traffic lights or buttons on a control pad.

Here are some examples of designs that help people with colour blindness:

The cards used by field hockey referees are different shapes.

Field hockey cards

Can you see how this control pad was designed so that colour blind users don't get confused?

Game controller

The crossing light uses different shapes.

Crossing light

Which Team?

What Adam sees.

Sometimes, when Adam plays football at school, it can be hard for him to tell who is on his team. He has to look really carefully to see the differences in the kits.

For the other players, it is really easy to tell who is on which team. Can you think of a way to make this match more <u>accessible</u> for people with colour blindness?

What Ján sees.

Professional football clubs are now thinking about how to make games more accessible for people with colour blindness.

OTHER TYPES OF COLOUR BLINDNESS

This book has looked at what it is like to have red-green colour blindness because most people who are colour blind have some type of red-green colour blindness, but there are other types.

Some people have blue-yellow colour blindness, and some are completely colour blind. Every person with colour blindness sees the world a little differently. Many scientists believe that it is a little different for everyone.

SUPPORT

If you think you might have colour blindness, you should talk to an adult. They can help you get a diagnosis.

If you have colour blindness, you might need some support. Adam's teacher supports him by having crayons that have the colour written on them. Adam's friend Ján helps him when they are doing tasks in class.

Even though people with colour blindness like Adam may see the world a little differently, we are more alike, all of us, than we are different.

GLOSSARY

accessible	being easily usable by people of different abilities
cells	the basic building blocks that make up all living things
condition	an illness or other medical problem
deficient	not having enough of something
designers	someone who plans how something that is going to be made will look and work
diagnosis	a decision about what an illness or condition is
professional	to do with a job that people who have special skills do
textures	the feel or appearance of an object's surface

INDEX

Adam 10–11, 14–15, 18, 22–23
bananas 14–15
blue 7–8, 12–13, 21
brains 13
control pads 16–17
cyan 13
designers 16
football 18–19
green 7–15, 20
help 12, 17, 22
inclusivity 16–17
Ján 10, 19, 22
yellow 7–8, 13, 15, 21